ONE OF THE BOYS

One of The Boys
Copyright © 2018 by Sean Morriseau

No part of this publication may be reproduced, distributed, or transmitted in any form or by any means, including photocopying, recording, or other electronic or mechanical methods, without the prior written permission of the author, except in the case of brief quotations embodied in critical reviews and certain other non-commercial uses permitted by copyright law.

Tellwell Talent
www.tellwell.ca

ISBN
978-1-77370-953-6 (Paperback)

It had just gotten dark out, and the sky was as clear as water.

"I can see the train tracks from here, make sure you have that bow ready," said Cody.

Moments later he shouted, "There he is I can see him! Harvey grab the wheel."

I struggled to keep the four-wheeler straight from the passenger's position, while Cody was lining up his shot with the bow. We were going about 60 km/h on a dirt road during the dark of the night. We were only feet away from the big **buck** that we had seen.

"River, Justin go around the fence and cut him off on the other side!" I yelled, while trying to keep the buck running in the same direction as the four-wheeler.

We were getting closer and closer on its ass, and all we could think about was the fried deer meat melting in our mouths. I remember the way my mom used to make it with fried bannock and mashed potatoes.

"Here's our chance boys. Steady now, steady!" cautioned Cody.

River and Justin came roaring from the other side of the fence, trapping the buck and leaving it no choice but to head for the bush.

"It's making a run for it!" yelled Justin.

"Shoot!" I screamed.

We watched the arrow release from the bow, as it soared into the darkness... until it was gone. We had all lost sight of the arrow.

"Did you hit it?" asked Justin, while scoping out the area.

"I don't know," replied Cody.

We drove up to the bush line and shined our lights on the trees.

"I see blood!" yelled River. "We got it."

We all cheered with satisfaction. Another kill with the bow! I wasn't sure how Cody did it, but he was like magic with that thing. It's like he's not even trying anymore.

"Just stick to driving there boys, no one can hunt like I do," Cody stated with a smirk on his face.

That's only because his father came from a family of hunters and fishers.

"We should probably get out of here before the RCMP find out we were hunting on private property again," said Justin. He was always the level headed one of the bunch.

We loaded up our kill onto the back of the four-wheeler and headed back to the rez. We all lived within footsteps of each other. It was a very small community. Justin was the white native. Always being picked on by the older community members for not fitting in. He had a lighter skin color, but he was just as aboriginal as we were. I guess that's what happens when your mom hooks up with a white guy. River was the quiet one when sober but the loud one when drunk. He didn't speak much unless he felt like it and for some reason he was always around, probably because he didn't have much family. Cody was the oldest out of the group. He always felt like he had more responsibility than us. When his dad left him at a young age he had no choice but to become the man of his house, while taking care of his little sisters. He ended up dropping out of school to put food on the table for his family. I look up to him, not many people can make those types of sacrifices. I come from a small family myself. My Mom died of breast cancer when I was 14, so now it's just Dad and I. We don't have much but we had enough to keep stable, most of the time. It wasn't always fun living in such a small community full of our closest cousins and friends. Somehow we managed to make it by each day.

We arrived back at Cody's house. His yard was always full of tools and broken down machines. Ever since his dad left he inherited all of his stuff. Things like his guns and his work shed. The shed was where we would hang our fresh kills, smoke and drink. We unloaded the buck off of the four-wheeler and hung it to drip. It was getting late out and tomorrow was a very important day for me, so we decided to call it a night and I headed home. I walked up my driveway passed the smashed up pick-up truck that's been sitting for years, rusting. I looked at the house, it used to be a beautiful home but is now falling apart from top to bottom. I realized that the lights were still on inside. It was almost two in the morning. My dad must have been drinking again. When I went inside, the house was quiet and my dad was passed out in the middle of the living room floor. He was like this every other night. A lot of things had changed, ever since the passing of my mother a year ago. I tossed a blanket on him and just left him there. I fried myself up some left overs that were in the fridge and started watching some movies. Trying to keep myself awake I stole a couple of smokes from my dad's room. He didn't care if I smoked, just as long as they weren't his smokes.

I ended up passing out right there on the couch. I didn't wake up until noon. I looked down and noticed that my dad was already gone. He must have headed out to see her already. His morning ritual was to visit her grave each day. I'm not sure where he goes after that, which is fine because he didn't care much about where I was. I didn't see him throughout the day anyway, we mostly just did our own things and stayed out of each other's way. There had been a lot of tension between us most days, I guess it's because we both grieve from the pain of our loss.

It was actually early for me. 1 o'clock was usually when I got up, mostly because I was up all night with the boys. I got myself dressed and headed out the door. I hated being at home because the house was always empty and it was always too quiet. I miss how mom would play music in the morning while she was cleaning, the smell of fresh breakfast in the air filling the house. It was a bright and sunny day outside. The type of day to put you in a good mood. I could tell mom was smiling right now. She always had a way of telling me she was there.

Three houses down was Cody's place. In his backyard was an old beat up camping trailer. It looked like shit and smelled even worse on the inside but that's where we usually meet up at and hangout most times. I walked into the trailer through a cloud of smoke.

"You want to hit this?" asked River.

He packed a glass pipe full of weed and handed it to me with a lighter. It wasn't my first time smoking weed and getting high. I took a hit from the pipe and sat down to enjoy the feeling. River always had his girlfriend Mandy around. She never really said much but she always had an extra smoke if you asked her for one.

The boys were talking about a pit party that was happening tonight down by the quarry just past the pipeline. The pipeline stretched far, all the way from the other side of the river where the town is, across our land and over into the American border. We were right in the middle and the quarry was just on the other side.

"How do you expect us to get there?!" I shouted from across the camper trailer.

"Well, your dad is never home and your mom's truck is just sitting there, and it hasn't been moved since…"

"Don't even say it. Too soon man." I stopped him before he could finish.

He was right, though. My dad put up a sign on the truck that said for sale… but I don't think anybody wants to buy that piece of shit rust bucket. I mean, it drives and all but it's not a bronco, that's for sure.

"Come on Harv, I can steal some booze from my uncle's place," said Justin.

I was down for it, but in the back of my mind I had a bit of a sick feeling. But, it wasn't anything some whiskey couldn't take away. We all wanted to eat first. After getting high, eating just made everything a whole lot better.

Cody's grandma always had food ready and she cooked for everyone. She helped the Elders and youth all the time and even catered community gatherings. She was the cook of the rez. It gave me a warm feeling every time we went to her house. The type of warm feeling that reminded me of my mom. I guess she was the only lady figure I had left in my life. We walked up the driveway and seen Cody's grandpa cleaning out his shed, which was full of feathers and guts. Right away we knew what grandma was cooking. She welcomed us into her house with a big smile and a warm bowl of partridge soup, fresh from this morning. It was like a bowl of heaven, steamy and delicious.

We headed over to Justin's house. His uncle always had a couple cases of Blue and a few bottles of whiskey in the fridge, which was in his garage. We knew that if we snuck into his garage without getting caught, we would be able to grab enough to drink for the pit party. We all stood at the edge of the road near the driveway while Justin slowly made his way to the garage. He came up to the side window and poked his head in to make sure it was empty. The coast was clear, he quickly ran around the side and rushed through the door. All we could hear from the road was the sound of metal banging and glass clinking. We looked to see if he was coming. Suddenly, Justin came running out of that garage door faster than a spooked deer.

"Holy, slow down there Buck," said Cody while laughing at Justin.

"Yah bud, you were like a buck running from a bullet in there," said River

Justin was able to make it out with a bottle of Jack and a few beers, as much as he could carry anyway. We all started calling him Buck after that. The way that boy runs when he is under pressure is too funny.

Now that we had our booze, we just needed some wheels. I still had that sick feeling in my stomach knowing that we were about to take my mom's truck. I wasn't sure if my dad was home. It was dinner time, so really, he could have been anywhere. I told the boys to load up the truck and get in the back. It was only a two-seater truck so two of us had to lay down in the box. I casually walked in, just in case my dad was home. I didn't see his boots at the door, so I knew he was still out somewhere. I also knew where he kept the keys to the truck, so I acted fast and got the hell out of there. I rushed to the truck and put the keys in the ignition.

"Let's hope she starts boys!" I yelled, while my heart was racing.

"Let's hope it has gas," laughed Cody from the box.

She turned over and luckily there was enough gas to get there and back. I pulled out of the driveway in my mom's old beater and headed towards the pipeline. I could hear Cody and Buck in the back already taking shots, yelling from the truck, "fuck you!" I could already tell it was going to be a crazy night. River blasted the radio and lit up a joint for the ride. We made our way past the pipeline, towards the quarry. We could see the fire from the middle of the dirt road. We weren't much further. We pulled up and parked on the bush line away from all the other vehicles, just in case the RCMP came. I didn't want them to confiscate my mom's truck. I got out and took my first shot right away. It burned but tasted great. We mostly knew everyone that was around. All cousins and close friends. It was like this every weekend, having big parties and getting drunk.

Everyone stood around the fire, it was huge. There were probably about 20 of us all around. We mostly huddled together and kept to ourselves, except River was always tied to his girl Mandy when he was drunk. I guess they had trust issues with each other. I didn't care much for having a girlfriend but I did get my fair share of action, not all girls in the community were my cousins. I was about 5 shots in and feeling pretty high from the weed. I could feel that my leash was about to break so I went for a walk to the truck to take a piss. Standing there, I could feel my buzz kicking in. I looked at my mom's truck and remembered the time she used to drive me to the community school. She only worked down the road at the band office, so she was able to pick me up when I got out of school. She was the reason I kept going. She would wake me up every morning and make breakfast, reminding me to brush my teeth. But now, I don't even know what day of the month it is half of the time. I finished my piss and made my way back to the fire. From where I was walking I could see a group of kids all huddled in a circle, chanting the word "fight". I ran up to get in on the action and realized that it was Buck fighting one of the older community members. At first I just sat back and watched it play out, but then I realized that Buck was getting it pretty bad so I quickly jumped in and pulled at the sweater of the other boy to throw him off. I thought for sure that he was going to hit me, but then one of the girls from the community stepped in and threw a drink in his face. I picked Buck up and we walked back to the fire.

"What the heck just happened, man?" asked Buck.

"I don't know, what were you fighting about anyway?" I asked, while lighting up a smoke for the both of us.

Buck said that the guy was talking shit about him from across the fire and kept egging him on, saying drunk comments, so Buck had enough of it and rushed him. The other boys weren't even around to witness the fight. Most likely messing around in the bush. The night was going by fast but before we knew it the bottle was empty and we only had a few beers left. Some of the other community members were even sniffing gasoline. I thought that was pretty stupid and I definitely wasn't drunk enough to try it. The crowd was getting smaller and the fire was dying out. Buck and I gathered up the boys and went to the truck. I was pretty drunk but I felt fine to drive and I wasn't letting any of those clowns behind the wheel. The boys all jumped in the back of the box while I sat alone up front. It was about a 10 minute drive down the dirt road before we get to the pipeline. It was pitch black outside and all you could see were the stars above. I was coming up a hill on the dirt road and I could see the lights from another vehicle shining from the opposite side. I knew there was another car coming, so I pulled off to the side and waited for it to pass me by. As soon as the driver saw my headlights, they must have hit their breaks pretty hard, because the car began to skid out of control. While it was coming over the top of the hill, it smashed right into the side of my mom's truck. It happened so fast, I didn't know how to react.

"Kick his ass!" yelled Cody, from the box of the truck.

"That was my first car accident," said River, he was numb from shock.

I tried to get out of the truck but my door was jammed shut. I got out through the passenger door and my first thought was, "what the fuck?". The front driver's wheel was pushed right in and flat, probably bent the frame of the truck. I looked over at the car that hit me, it was only a small car and barley took any damage. Just a dented front bumper and smashed lights. Thankfully the driver was alone and he wasn't hurt. I was still in shock when he got out of his car. My first reaction was to hug him and make sure he was alright. I didn't know who he was and I didn't really care, I was just mad about the truck and I knew I was going to get shit from my dad. We had no choice but leave the crash site and come back for the truck in the morning. If we were to call a tow truck now they would call the RCMP on us for drinking and driving. The rez was only about an hour away on foot, we still had a couple drinks left so we gathered up everything from the truck and started to head home.

The next morning I woke up pretty early. That sick feeling I had came back again. I knew my dad was going to ask about the truck so I was just going to tell him. He didn't get as mad as I thought he was going to, which was odd because normally he would have welted my ass with a belt. It was almost as if he didn't even care about the truck anymore. He didn't even try to get it out of the bush.

"Ah, just fucking leave it there," he said.

At that moment I never felt more alone than I did when mom died. I was mad at him but I was too scared show it. He never showed care for me like he used too, so I stopped caring about him.

After that day, my dad and I never really talked. Our connection as father and son had faded to nothing but a lost memory. As the days went by, the more trouble I found myself in. I wasn't into school anymore. My teachers even stopped calling the house. I was never quite the worker either and most people didn't want to hire me anyway. We were known as the bad kids in the community. No one ever really gave me a chance so I turned to the only way I knew to make fast money. On the rez, that was by stealing and selling. We started stealing bikes, shoes, clothes, groceries and gas. We even started selling weed and the money started coming and going.

We had a plan to go steal some groceries from the stores in town. The price of food on the rez is expensive and most people can't afford to buy enough groceries, so we sell for a cheaper price. We headed out on foot, River and his girlfriend Mandy stayed back to sell weed out of the camper trailer. That's where most of our customers would come to pick up. It wasn't too far of a walk to the closest town, so we decided to car hop along the way, going in and out of vehicles. We were looking for things like wallets and loose change. It was one of the easiest ways of making money and fast. It was getting dark outside, so it was the perfect time to do it. I spotted my first car sitting in a driveway with no one around. I walked up to the car and pulled the handle to see if it was locked. It opened up, so I sat down and closed the door, treating it as if it were my own vehicle. Quickly, I searched through all the compartments and cup holders of the car, filling my pockets with anything that I could grab. It was dim on the inside, so I couldn't see much. I jumped out of the car as fast as I could and met up with the boys, who were around the corner.

"Anything good in there?" asked Buck, "Or is it just shit?"

All that was in the car was $7 in change, a pack of smokes, a lighter and some old paper slips. It was a good start but there were more cars to be hit up. It was getting darker outside and the next vehicle was sitting right under a street light. It was a black car with tinted windows.

"I got this one," said Cody, "keep a look out for me."

Buck and I watched from the bushes on the other side of the street. Cody slowly made his way up to the car to see if it was open. As soon as he pulled the handle an alarm went off. I saw Cody run towards us but Buck and I ran further into the bush to get away from the area. We ended up losing Cody and meeting up with him outside the grocery store.

"Where did you boys go?" asked Cody. "I almost shit my pants back there."

"You try keeping up with Buck. The kid just ran," I replied.

We were just lucky we didn't get caught. I was feeling hesitant about hitting up the grocery store, but I knew in my mind there was a lot of money to be made. All we had to do was bring our own grocery bags from home, walk into the store with a cart each and fill the bags up. Quickly, while no one is looking, we make our way through the exit one at a time like we just paid for everything. That was the plan. It was easier said than done. We made our way into the store and split up. I grabbed a basket so I didn't have to carry so many items back to the camper trailer. It wasn't my first time stealing food but every time I did, my hands would shake and my palms would get all sweaty. I remember going grocery shopping with my mom when I was just a boy. Every Sunday she would take me with her. She would always buy the same things; flour, eggs, oil and yeast. I remember because that's what she used to make her bannock with.

I started to fill my bag with mostly meat, including pork and beef. It was the most expensive, so we made a little more selling it. I even filled my bag with bottles of water because clean water wasn't cheap and I know a lot of elders who would pay a lot just for a bottle. I finished filling my bag and started to head to the exit. Before I was able to make my way through I heard a voice behind me yell.

"Stop that kid!"

Right away I dropped my basket and put my hands up. I watched Cody run past me with a full cart of groceries, right to the rim of the buggy. Security chased him through the first door of the store and then grabbed Cody by his jacket, throwing him into the window and dragging him back into the store. I didn't know what to do. I was standing right next to the exit where Cody was caught. I tried to act like I didn't know him and just walk out with my basket, but then an old lady who witnessed us came into the store shaking her finger at me.

"That's his friend!" she scowled.

"Fuck you lady!" I yelled at her, while giving her a mean look. They took me and Cody to the back of the store and sat us down on an old dirty carpet in some office.

"We take meat theft very seriously here," said the store owner.

I couldn't help but laugh when he said that. I looked over at Cody and realized that it was just us two. Buck must have been the first one to leave the store because he got away, that lucky bastard, the old lady must not have seen him walk in with us. We waited for the RCMP to arrive. It took them almost an hour just to get to the grocery store. The owner wasn't happy with us but he didn't want to press charges. He just didn't want us back in his store ever again. He got the RCMP to write up a couple of trespassing orders against Cody and I. They said if we were to step foot on the grocery store property ever again we would be charged for trespassing. The owner took both of our pictures and contact information. The RCMP walked us out of the store and drove us back to the rez. We were lucky to get away ourselves. I was pissed off because I knew that was a lot of money gone down the drain. It gives me anxiety thinking about where our next big score was going to come from.

I met up with River and Mandy at the camper, at least they were able to make a couple of dollars selling a few bags. When I got inside Buck was sitting there with a smile on his face.

"What happened to you boys?" asked Buck, "I came back for you guys and seen cops outside the store."

I explained to him what happened, that we got kicked out of the store for good. He only got away with a few things himself. He sold all his shit for a pack of smokes and $60. He didn't even cut us in either or come back to see if we were okay. We took a break for the night and decided to just have some drinks and smoke up. I was still a little shook from being busted. I didn't want to head back out there again on the same night. That would be crazy. We all got fucked up like we usually did and just crashed out in the camper. I woke to the smell of puke, empty bottles and cigarette butts scattered over the floor. I felt like shit and I was starving. I looked over at River and he had a big black dick drawn right on the side of his face and other shit written all over his body. It was just us two in the camper. I got out to take a piss and Cody and Buck were still drinking outside next to the fire pit.

"What a fucking night, eh boys?" asked Buck, "Just rough."

It was already lunch time but the day had just started for me. I cracked open a beer and joined the boys next to the fire.

"So what's the plan today?" I asked. "Where we going to get money from next?"

After being caught from stealing form the grocery store, we didn't have much options left. Nothing we can do in the day light anyway. We decided to go hunting to clear our minds and get some food. Buck pulled out the old .22 rifle from Cody's dad's old gun box and we hopped on the four-wheelers. We took off across the train tracks. We drove along the pipeline because that's where we saw the most partridge. They were easy to kill and easy to clean. We also would set up snares along the bush line of the trail so we could catch rabbits and foxes. It was a beautiful afternoon with the sun shining in our faces. We only spotted a couple birds but that's all we really needed to eat for the day. I shot one of them and Cody shot the rest.

We made our way back to Cody's house to clean the birds and cook them up. I was still thinking about how we could make some more money. I was pacing the back yard while I was eating my fresh kill. I always get this anxious feeling when I'm not doing something that involved stealing. I hated living in such a small community where everyone knew everyone and everything was expensive. It was getting dark outside. I was getting tired of just sitting around smoking weed and burning out. Cody came up with an idea. He wanted to steal the bingo money from the community. The elders in the community always left the bingo money in the community center office. There's probably about $1000 sitting there right now.

"How are we going to break into the community center?" I asked Cody.

The only way in and out of the building was through the front and back door and they both get locked up every night at the same time. The elders who are in charge of the community center don't even let us inside because we stole all the ash trays that belonged to the bingo hall... and got caught. I wasn't too sure about Cody's idea of stealing all the bingo money but I also didn't want to seem like a little bitch in front of the boys. It was still dark outside so Cody wanted to act fast. We knew nobody was at the community center at this time of the night, so we made our way there without really planning on what we were going to do when we arrived. I knew for sure the only way in was through a window but it wasn't going to be easy. We scouted the area from a distance before approaching the building. It was Cody, Buck and I. There was no one in sight and no vehicles around. We ran up to the side of the building to the window where the office was. We were sure the money was in there but we weren't sure how to get in. Buck checked to see if any of the windows were open but none of them were. I went around the other side of the building to check the other windows and still none of them were open. I ran back to the other side, when I turned the corner I seen Cody throw a rock right into the window of the office.

"What the heck are you doing?" I yelled softly.

"Shut up and keep watch Harvey," replied Cody, as he jumped through the window.

Buck followed him inside and I ran to the bush to watch from there. Before I could even get to the bush line I heard an alarm go off behind me in the community center. The boys were still inside. I yelled for them to run but they were taking too long. That sick feeling in my stomach started to come back again. I didn't know what to do so I just ran. I ran back to the camper. I ran into the camper so fast I almost broke the door down.

"What the fucks going on?" asked River who was sitting there in the camper with his girlfriend Mandy.

I didn't know what was happening. I told him that Cody and Buck smashed a window at the community center and broke in before the alarm started to go off. I wasn't sure if they got out of there or not. I explained to River that I was trying to yell for them to get out of there but I got scared and ran off. I was worried about them but I wasn't heading back out there. River and I just sat in the camper and waited to see if the boys were going to show up. Not too long into waiting we heard sirens in the distance. It must be the RCMP. As we waited the sirens got closer and then they stopped. I heard a car door close outside the camper.

"Come out with your hands up!" yelled an RCMP officer.

I didn't know what to think, my heart dropped into my stomach. I thought about running but realized that we were in a camper trailer with only one door.

"I'm walking out Harv," said River, shaking from head to toe.

I knew there was no other way out. We were probably surrounded. Cody and Buck probably snitched us out. I picked up a cigarette and lit it, than I walked out of the camper with my hands on my head.

"Get down on the ground!" yelled the Officer. "Put your hands behind your back."

They arrested us. There were three cars and about six RCMP Officers. They raided the camper and found our stash of money and weed. They also got me on camera as an accomplice with the boys breaking into the community center. When I asked the officer where Cody and Buck were he said that I wouldn't be seeing them for a long time. This didn't make my situation any better knowing that I just got into trouble with the RCMP the other day for shop lifting. They separated River and I and drove us to the DJ, The District Jail.

It was almost morning. They put me in a tiny room with a cement slab for a bed and a metal shitter with no toilet paper. I tried to get some sleep but I couldn't. I had that sick feeling. I knew this time we were fucked. I kept thinking about my mom and the times she would slap me in the head when I came home in trouble or got a phone call from school because I was giving the teachers a hard time. She would always straighten me out. Now, I'm sitting in jail and my dad doesn't know or care where I am. I sat there until the sun came up, thinking about how it would have been if she hadn't died. If she was still here, would I be here right now? I know things would have been different for sure, because she gave me hope.

I heard the door open and an officer walk down the hall. It was time for my trial. I didn't know what to expect. The hand cuffs were cold and tight, I could feel them cutting into my wrists. I thought to myself that I'd do anything to get out of here. When I was standing in front of the judge I felt so ashamed of myself, I couldn't even look her in the eye but I had no choice. I stood there as she read off the list of crimes I committed. I thought for sure I was going away but because of my young age and the fact that I only committed a small crime she let me go with 500 hours of community service and probation. I was set free. I felt blessed. I knew my mother must have been up there praying for me. I promised the judge that I would do better and I thanked her for taking it easy on me. I was told to report to the probation office to pick up my letter of community service. I didn't know what they were going to give me but anything was better than jail. I was introduced to Nancy, my probation officer. She told me a little bit about herself but everything she needed to know about me was in my file. She's a kind, bigger lady with a warm smile. She almost reminded me of my mother but only younger. When she asked what my father did for a living I told her that I didn't really see him much. He was a drunk always trying to pick a fight with me. She knew my mother died of cancer but never seemed to bring it up in front of me. I guess she thought it would make me mad but I'm over that stage of my life. She assigned me to work in the elder's home with the old and sick elders of our community.

"I'm not changing some old guy's diaper," I explained bluntly.

"No Harvey, You will be there to help take care of them emotionally and help support them in physical activities," replied Nancy, while laughing.

She assured me that that job involved hard work but was full of fun and excitement. How fun could it be spending eight hours a day with someone's grandpa? I guess I didn't really have a choice. I started immediately the next day. Every week I have to report my hours to Nancy and prove to her that I am going to my community service. It didn't seem so hard. If I steal a car I could manage to show up once a week.

I was driven home from the P.O by an RCMP officer because they weren't able to get ahold of my dad while I was in jail. When I walked into my house it was no surprise that he was gone and the house was a mess. Even the fridge was empty and I was starving. The first thing I did was take a nice long shower. I haven't been home in a few days, so I've been wearing the same clothes and I stunk. I wasn't sure what happened to the rest of the boys. I haven't seen any of them since we were all separated. I'm not sure if the judge gave them the same penalty as she gave me. I went over to Cody's house. When I got to his yard I seen that the camper was gone. That place was like my second home. I walked up to Cody's and knocked on the door. His mother answered looking like she had been crying all night. She slapped me across the face and told me to go home.

"Go home Harvey, just go home!" she yelled with anger and sadness in her voice.

I didn't know how to react. The sting of her hand fresh on my face. She's never treated me like that before. I could feel that she was hurt but what did I do to deserve that? I started walking back down to the rez and I saw Mandy walking her dog by herself. I ran up to her to ask if she's seen River but she told me that River and she were no longer together. She told me he was okay but she was mad at us for fucking up. She told me that Cody was in jail and that he got 2 years before he is ever going to get out again. Buck got sent to a boy's home out west for teenagers with behavior issues. I was shocked how they got such harsh penalties and I got away so easy. I wasn't the only one. River only got community service as well but Mandy told me that he's in so much trouble with his parents that we are not even allowed to see him anymore. His parents got him tied down with a leash now. I was the only one without any real support. I guess you could say I'm all alone. I parted ways with Mandy and it was probably the last time I was ever going to see her. She never really talked much and just always hung around the camper like a burn out.

The next day I got ready to start my first day of community service. My first day at the elder's home. I always start the day off with a smoke and a toke but I didn't have weed, all the boys were gone and I did not know where to get any. I was lucky I didn't have to get tested for drugs on a regular basis but it didn't matter because I didn't have any drugs to smoke. I arrived at the elder's home just a little late. I was never good at attendance in school and I always found it hard to pay attention to the time wherever I went. On the inside it was almost like a hotel. There was a lobby, only instead of children running around there were old people sitting around smoking. It smelt like a hospital, even worse. I checked in at the front desk where I was given information on my tasks for each day. They assigned me to take care of one of the elders. I didn't have any experience taking care of someone before, let alone an old man, but it was better than jail. I made my way through the smoke filled halls of the elder's home. It was a very grey and dull place with nothing to offer... until I heard a sound I've never heard before. It was coming from the end of the hall. Distracted by the beautiful music that struck my ears, I followed the sound to see what is was. I walked into the room the music was coming from and there it was. It was even more fascinating in person. I've heard guitars play through songs on the radio but never before in front of me. The sound was so amazing it had me tapping my feet. It gave me a warm feeling inside like my mom was in the room. I stood there and watched until the elder was done playing.

"Come on in," said the elder, "you must be my helper."

It turned out that he was the elder I was to be looking after. I stood there at the door with nothing to say. I was shy. He spoke first and told me his name. Bear. I walked in and sat in the corner. His room was small.

"So, do you have a name?" Bear asked while putting away his guitar.

"Harvey, my name is Harvey," I replied, with a shy tone in my voice.

I wasn't sure what to do. I had never had a job before and taking care of elders didn't really seem like any work until a nurse walked in with a wheelchair. It belonged to Bear. I was shocked to see that he was unable to walk but he told me not to look so surprised.

"I've been in a wheelchair my whole life," he said, "now help me get into this thing."

I wasn't sure how to help, but I tried to pick him up anyway. Suddenly he yelled and told me to stop. I stood back as he struggled to get himself into his chair. He seemed to have a grumpy side to him. It was lunch time in the elder's home so it was my job to make sure that Bear got to the lunch hall and was fed. I wheeled him out of his room and brought him to sit with the other elders while we waited for his meal, but I noticed he didn't like socializing with the others. He just wanted to be outside in the fresh air away from all the cigarette smoke. I just wanted to have a smoke. There was nobody around that was my age and everyone else who worked there were just as dull as the elders. I felt out of place, I even started having second thoughts of jail but remembered that I was to go home after. In jail your home is four concrete walls and a slab to sleep on. I was bored already and it was only day one. The food came out warm and mashed. I wasn't sure what it was but it didn't look good to eat. I could tell Bear was sick of eating as well.

Lunch was short and depressing. We made our way to the culture room where the afternoon activities took place; such as beading and drumming. It was hard for me to get Bear to participate in any of the social gatherings but he did enjoy painting by himself. He didn't mind my company. I even sat next to him and started to paint myself, I was never much of an artist but I enjoyed expressing myself on paper. I asked Bear if he had any family but he never replied. He just sort of grunted it off and kept on painting. He had a ring on his finger but I wasn't going to ask him if he was married. I'm sure he has friends that come to visit him from time to time. The day went on faster than I thought, maybe it was because I was late but I was happy it was over. I told Bear I would see him tomorrow. He didn't say anything but just waved his hand and closed the door on me. I knew it was going to be a long couple of weeks.

I had a lot of free time on my hands after community service. No one was ever really around to hang out with. All the boys were gone and the rez was so small, there was nowhere to go. I went to visit Cody in the district jail. It wasn't too far of a bus ride from where I lived. When I arrived at the jail I had to sign in and tell the officer at the front office who I was there to visit. I also had to hand over any illegal objects or items I may have had on me but I wasn't carrying anything. It took about 15 minutes for Cody to get to the visiting area. They put us in a room with a glass wall between us and a phone to communicate. He looked the same only with his head shaven and dressed in an orange jump suit. I picked up the phone on my end but he just sat there with his arms crossed, staring at me. He was mad at me. I could tell because I've known him my whole life. I was about to put my phone down but then he picked his phone up and the first thing he said was that it was my fault he was in there. Right away I got mad just for him thinking that. I thought, why the fuck would it be my fault I wasn't the one who smashed the window and broke in? He was mad because when they got out of the building that day I wasn't there. He thought that I had ditched him that night and just took off, but he didn't know that I was screaming for them to get out.

"It's your fault that you're in here!" I yelled through the phone, "not mine."

He threw his phone at the glass window without even putting it back on the hook. He got up and asked to be taken back to his cell. I felt so angry, someone I use to look up to was accusing me for his own actions. Fuck him, I thought. I tried to be nice and come visit a friend and I get shit on in return. I wasn't going to come back and see him again, if he really cared he wouldn't have been an asshole.

I made my way home. It was getting late outside, so the bus ride back to the rez was quiet and empty. When I got home my dad was actually there. He didn't have a single clue what happened to me or what I went through but he was still being an asshole. It was hard for me to keep my distance from him. When

I walked in he was crying. It was not from being drunk though, he was actually sad. He told me he was sorry. I didn't know if he was drunk or not, but I felt his pain and I started to cry. I never hugged my dad since the funeral back when things were normal but when he hugged me it made me feel like a different person. It made me feel like a man. I never thought I would have this moment with my dad again and I wasn't sure if it was temporary or not, but I took advantage of the moment and told him that I loved him. After all it was only the two of us.

The next day I went to community service. I wasn't late this time. When I walked in I heard that sound again. It was playing so beautifully through the halls of the elder's home. I knew Bear was playing his guitar. The sound drew me right into his room. I watched him sit there as he played his guitar with such experience and emotion. It was like every tune he played told a story about his life. The guitar looked so beautiful, it was made of wood with a painted feather. I could tell Bear painted it himself. He stopped playing and put it away. I wasn't sure if he liked people watching him play but I loved watching him.

"Are you ready for today?" Bear asked as he was closing up his guitar case.

He seemed much happier than he did yesterday. I could tell because he wasn't grunting as much. The day went on but the hours were going by slowly. All day I was thinking about how well Bear was playing his guitar. The music coming from such a small piece of wood was just magical. I couldn't help but want to hear more. I was too shy to ask Bear to pull it out again thinking it would make him mad. It was just after lunch and Bear and I made our way back to his room. Bear normally used the washroom after lunch, that's one thing I didn't have to help him with. I thought about taking a look at his guitar while I had a chance. I pulled it out and opened the case. It was so shiny that I didn't even want to touch it but I wanted to learn how to play. I was about to pick it up but then Bear came back into the room.

"Put that down!" he yelled, "get out of here!"

I was so startled that I dropped his guitar case causing his guitar to fall out onto the floor. I ran out of the room as fast as I could without even picking it up. I felt so bad that I had went home early, even though it would cut back on my hours for my community service. I was scared to go back and see Bear, but thankfully the next day was a Saturday and I didn't have community service on weekends. I had to report my hours to Nancy every Sunday and tell her how my community service was going. She already knew about the incident that happened with Bear and his guitar. It was an honest mistake I shouldn't have made. Nancy was more upset with the lack of hours I was putting in each day. I was behind and if I didn't catch up soon I could possibly go to jail.

"You can do it Harvey," Nancy always said.

She always encouraged me and was nice about it, never getting mad but just upset. She knew I was more than just a bad kid. She just wanted to see me do better.

I was nervous to see Bear again. I wanted to make things better between him and I so when I went to see him again. I brought him some bannock from my mom's recipe. I knew it would be better than to eat the food they served at the elder's home. I also wrote him a letter, apologizing for touching his guitar. I wanted to get on his good side since I was going to be with him for a couple more weeks. I got to the elder's home and thought I would walk into the sound of Bear playing again, but it was quiet. When I got to his room he was just sitting there while playing cards.

"Good morning Bear," I said with a smile on my face.

I placed my apology letter on the table in front of him. He didn't read it so I just left it there for him just in case he wanted to read it later. I offered him a piece of bannock. I knew he wouldn't be able to resist such a tasty snack before lunch. He took it from me and started eating it right away. I could see by the look in his eyes that it brought him back to his childhood. He told me he hadn't had a piece of bannock that good since his wife was still alive. It reminded him of her. I could tell he was happy. I saw a tear run down his face as he finished his last bite. I knew why he was so grumpy, I would be too if I was all alone. I tried my best to get to know him all day while I had him in a good mood. He told me a lot about his life before the elder's home. That he used to travel from community to community teaching others about our culture. He was into everything: beading, drumming, singing and more. I was fascinated by his stories and how he was able to do so much without the use of his legs. He told me about his wife and how she passed away from cancer, just like my mom did. I felt that we were the same in some ways, both with a rough past. The day went by faster than any other. We got along better than we did before and I promised him I would bring him a piece of bannock every day.

The next day I came in early to see Bear. When I walked into his room he had his guitar out on the bed.

"I read your letter," Bear said, "Do you want to learn how to play?"

He knew I was interested in his guitar. I never had a chance to learn anything before and no one had ever really offered to teach me how to play.

"Go ahead, pick it up," he said.

The guitar was lighter than I thought it would be. I strummed the guitar from top to bottom. It was my first time ever playing an instrument and it felt amazing. I wanted to learn how to play like Bear. I wanted to make my own music.

He started to teach me the basics of how to play. How to hold the guitar, where to put your fingers and which way to strum. It was so much harder than it looked. Trying to match each rhythm and sound, but I was so happy that Bear and I were getting along and that he was teaching me how to play. I started feeling less like the bad kid everyone seen me as and started feeling like someone who mattered.

I focused every day on my community service and learned how to play the guitar. I was actually eager to wake up every morning and head to the elder's home. I even ended up quitting smoking weed because it would just make me lazy and sleep all the time. I stopped thinking about the boys too. I knew that they were the reason I was being dragged down in life. I started taking care of myself better and started visiting mom again. I just wish my dad would do the same and get off his ass. Perhaps find himself a job. He still drinks but we don't fight as much as we used to. My mom was always on my mind everywhere I went. I felt like when I was playing the guitar I was playing it for her and the more I learned the more she was with me. Even Nancy started to notice a difference in my behavior. My weekly reports with her were going great. My hours were all caught up and I was getting close to the end of my community service.

It was my last week at the elder's home. My hours were almost complete. I felt like a new person. I even started opening Bear up to the other elders. Before he was just a cranky old man who didn't care to talk to anyone. It was almost as if he hated himself, but together we overcame our problems and it made us better people. There was still so much Bear wanted to teach me and I loved spending time with him. I almost didn't want my community service to end. Thankfully, I knew I was able to come visit him whenever I wanted.

When I came to see him on my last day, I had brought him a whole basket of bannock. I knew for sure he was going to like it. I also wrote him another letter thanking him for all he taught me. When I got to the elder's home, the lobby was empty and not a person was in sight. I made my way to Bear's room but when I got there it was empty. All of his stuff was gone. His bed was made and his room was clean. The chairs were all tucked in and his pictures were gone. The only thing left was his guitar and a note sitting there in the middle of the room.

Dear Harvey,

I'm glad we've gotten to know each other over the past couple of weeks. You really made me a happy man. I know about everything that you've done and everything that you went through. I talk to Nancy on a regular basis and I want you to know that you're not a bad person. You're just a good kid who made stupid choices, but it's time for you to grow up. I never told you this, but I've been sick for a while now and my time is coming to an end, so I wrote you this letter in hopes that it gets to you when I'm gone. Remember where you come from and who you are. Follow your passion and stick to your culture. I want you to have this guitar and remember me every time you play it. I want you to keep playing it and maybe one day someone will find you and they will want to learn just as much as you did. You have something special and no one can ever take that away from you. I hope you make smart choices and remember why we met.

Take care friend, Bear.

Bear died the night before from kidney failure. Even though he was gone, I still brought him a piece of bannock every day when I went to visit mom and I played his guitar for him just like he showed me. I was no longer one of the boys. I was a man.

ABOUT THE AUTHOR

I WAS BORN in Vancouver, British Columbia in 1994. I would say I come from a mid-sized family. It was Mom, Dad, Nicole, Stephanie, James and I. We didn't have much growing up but we always had each other. I moved to Fort William First Nation, Ontario when I was about 5 years old. It's where my dad was originally born and is now my pride and home. I grew up on the rez and did a lot for someone my age. Most of the events in my book are based on true experiences that have happened to me and my community growing up. I'm still young and I have a lot to learn but everyday is a new adventure for me. I enjoy my culture and where I come from and I'm proud to say that I'm indigenous.

www.ingramcontent.com/pod-product-compliance
Lightning Source LLC
LaVergne TN
LVHW011900060526
838200LV00054B/4454